FAVORITE MOTHER GOOSE RHYMES

Mary Had a Little Lamb

Distributed by The Child's World®
1980 Lookout Drive • Mankato, MN 56003-1705
800-599-READ • www.childsworld.com

Acknowledgments
The Child's World®: Mary Berendes, Publishing Director
The Design Lab: Kathleen Petelinsek, Design

Library of Congress Cataloging-in-Publication Data
Hale, Sarah Josepha Buell, 1788-1879.
Mary had a little lamb / illustrated by Liza Woodruff.
p. cm.
ISBN 978-1-60954-281-8 (library bound: alk. paper)
1. Lambs—Juvenile poetry. 2. Nursery rhymes, American. 3. Children's poetry, American. I. Woodruff, Liza, ill. II. Title.
PS1774.H2M3 2011b
811'.2—dc22 2010032416

Printed in the United States of America in Mankato, Minnesota.
December 2010
PA02073

ILLUSTRATED BY LIZA WOODRUFF

Mary had a little lamb.
Its fleece was white as snow.

And everywhere that Mary went,
the lamb was sure to go.

It followed her to school one day—
that was against the rule.
It made the children
laugh and play
to see a lamb at school.

And so the teacher turned it out,
but still it lingered near,
and waited patiently about
till Mary did appear.

"Why does the lamb love Mary so?"
the eager children cry.

"Why, Mary loves the lamb,
you know!" the teacher did reply.

MATH

ABOUT MOTHER GOOSE

We all remember the Mother Goose nursery rhymes we learned as children. But who was Mother Goose, anyway? Did she even exist? The answer is . . . we don't know! Many different tales surround this famous name.

Some people think she might be based on Goose-footed Bertha, a kindly old woman in French legend who told stories to children. The inspiration for this legend might have been Queen Bertha of France, who died in 783 and whose son Charlemagne ruled much of Europe. Queen Bertha was called Big-footed Bertha or Queen Goosefoot because one foot was larger than the other.

The name "Mother Goose" first appeared in Charles Perrault's *Les Contes de ma Mère l'Oye* ("Tales of My Mother Goose"), published in France in 1697. This was a collection of fairy tales including "Cinderella" and "Sleeping Beauty"—but these were stories, not poems. The first published Mother Goose nursery rhymes appeared in England in 1781, as *Mother Goose's Melody; or Sonnets for the Cradle*. But some of the verses themselves are hundreds of years old, passed along by word of mouth.

Although we don't really know the origins of Mother Goose or her nursery rhymes, we *do* know that these timeless verses are beloved by children everywhere!

ABOUT THE ILLUSTRATOR

Liza Woodruff has been illustrating children's books for thirteen years. She lives in Vermont in an old farmhouse with her husband, two children, a cat, a dog, two guinea pigs, and three chickens. Liza is constantly inspired by her children and pets, and the farm country where they all live.